The
Secret Garden

My First Classics

A Little Princess

by Frances Hodgson Burnett,

adapted by Laura F. Marsh

My First Classics

The Secret Garden

BY FRANCES HODGSON BURNETT

ADAPTED BY LAURA F. MARSH

HarperFestival®

A Division of HarperCollinsPublishers

HarperCollins®, ☰®, and HarperFestival® are trademarks of
HarperCollins Publishers, Inc.

My First Classics: The Secret Garden
© 2005 by HarperCollins Publishers
Printed in the United States of America. For information address
HarperCollins Children's Books, a division of HarperCollins
Publishers, 1350 Avenue of the Americas, New York, NY 10019.
www.harperchildrens.com
Library of Congress catalog card number: 2004111658
Typography by Tom Starace
1 2 3 4 5 6 7 8 9 10
❖
First HarperFestival edition, 2005

Contents

The
Secret Garden

There's No One Left

When Mary Lennox came to live with her uncle at Misselthwaite Manor in England, everyone said she was a most unpleasant-looking child. She was very thin, with yellow skin and a sour expression. She had lived in India and was often sick.

Mary's father worked for the English government and was a busy man. Her mother was a beautiful woman and only wanted to go to parties. She hadn't wanted a daughter. So when Mary was born, an *ayah*, an Indian nurse, cared for Mary. The *ayah* was told to keep Mary out of the way.

Mary spent all of her time with her *ayah* and the other servants. She was always given her way and became a very selfish little girl.

One hot morning when Mary was about nine years old, she awoke to find a servant by her bed. When Mary asked for her *ayah*, the servant looked frightened and said that her *ayah* could not come. Mary threw herself into a fit, but the woman only repeated what she had said.

Something strange was happening. Several servants were missing and those who Mary saw hurried about with scared faces. Mary played by herself for a long time. Later she saw her mother talking with an officer on the porch. Mary's mother usually had large, laughing eyes. But today her mother's eyes were not laughing.

"Is it so very bad?" her mother asked him.

"Awfully, Mrs. Lennox," he said. "You should have gone to the hills two weeks ago."

"Oh, I know I should have! What a fool I was!"

There was a loud wailing from the servants' quarters. Mary's mother clutched the officer's arm.

"What is it?" she gasped.

"Someone has died," he answered. "You did not say it had broken out among your servants."

"I did not know!" she cried. "Come!" And she turned and ran into the house.

Thereafter it was explained to Mary that the terrible disease of cholera had broken out and people were dying quickly. Her *ayah* had gotten sick overnight and had died. Three other servants were dead and others had run away in fear.

During the confusion of the second day, Mary hid in the nursery and was forgotten by everyone. She heard strange sounds of wailing and hurrying feet. Mary cried and slept through the hours. When she got hungry, she crept to the dining room and found a half-eaten meal on the table. She ate it and soon fell asleep again.

Mary slept so soundly that she did not hear the sounds of things being carried out of the bungalow. When she awakened, the house was silent. She was not an affectionate child and never cared much for anyone.

When her *ayah* died, she did not cry. She wondered only who would take care of her now. If everyone had gotten well again, surely someone would come look for her.

But no one came. As Mary lay waiting, the house seemed to become more and more silent. After quite a long time, she heard footsteps. No servant went to meet them, and she heard people entering the house, opening doors, and looking into rooms.

"What a sad place!" she heard one voice say. "That pretty woman! And I suppose the child, too, but no one saw her."

Mary was standing in the middle of the nursery when they opened the door a few minutes later.

"Barney!" the officer cried out. "There is a child here! A child alone—in a place like this! Mercy on us, who is she?"

"I am Mary Lennox," Mary said, standing tall and looking quite cross. "I fell asleep when everyone got sick. Why does no one come?" Mary stamped her foot stubbornly.

The young officer whose name was Barney looked at her sadly. Mary thought he blinked away tears.

"Poor child!" he said. "There is nobody left to come."

It was a strange way for Mary to find out that she had neither a mother nor a father left. They had died and been carried away in the night. The few servants who survived left the house quickly. None of them remembered Mary. That was why the house was so quiet. Mary was the only one left.

~ 2 ~

The Journey to England

Mary knew so little of her parents that she did not miss them when they were gone. Her only thought was for herself.

She was told she was going to live with her uncle, Mr. Archibald Craven, at Misselthwaite Manor in England. Mary made the long trip on a ship with an officer's wife who looked after her. When they arrived in London, her uncle's housekeeper, Mrs. Medlock, met her at the ship.

Right away Mary didn't like Mrs. Medlock. This was not unusual since she rarely liked anybody. Mary had overheard the two women talking about how yellow and sour she looked. "Her mother was so beautiful and had fine manners. She is nothing like her mother," they said.

The next day Mary got on a train with Mrs. Medlock. "I suppose I should tell you about where you are going. You are going to a strange place," the housekeeper said.

Mary said nothing, so Mrs. Medlock continued.

"The house is six hundred years old, and it's on the

edge of a moor. There are one hundred rooms in it. Most of them are locked. And there's a lawn around it with gardens."

Mary was listening, but she did not want to look interested.

"Well, what do you think?" asked Mrs. Medlock.

"Nothing," said Mary. "It doesn't matter what I think."

"You are right about that," she replied. "Mr. Craven never troubles himself about anyone." Then she appeared to remember something. "He has a crooked back. He was a sour young man, and didn't make use of his money until he was married."

Mary had heard Mr. Craven was a hunchback and she was surprised he was married. When Mary's eyes turned toward Mrs. Medlock, the housekeeper went on.

"She was a sweet, pretty woman, and he would have done anything for her. When she died—"

Mary jumped a little. "Oh, did she die?" Mary exclaimed, without meaning to. It made her feel suddenly sorry for Mr. Archibald Craven.

"Yes," said Mrs. Medlock. "And it made him stranger than ever. He won't see people. Most of the time he is away, but when he is at home, he shuts himself up in his rooms."

It sounded like something in a book, and it did not make Mary feel cheerful. Mrs. Medlock spoke again.

"You shouldn't expect to see Mr. Craven, or that there will be people to talk to. You'll play and look after yourself. You'll be told which rooms you can go into. But when you are in the house, don't go searching around. He won't like it."

Mary stopped feeling sorry for Mr. Craven because he sounded so unpleasant. She looked out the window and let her eyes fall slowly shut.

~ 3 ~

Across the Moor

Mary awoke to Mrs. Medlock speaking. "It's time to wake up. We're at the station and we've got a long drive ahead of us."

When they got off the train, a carriage stood waiting for them. Mary looked into the night, curious about what she would see. She had lived her whole life in India and did not know what to expect in England.

"What is a moor?" she asked suddenly.

"You'll see it in about ten minutes," Mrs. Medlock said.

Mary saw a tiny village. They passed hedges and trees and then there was nothing for a long time.

"Eh! We're on the moor now," said Mrs. Medlock.

They were on a rough road with bushes on either side. But it was dark as far as she could see. The wind was rising and making a wild, low, rushing sound.

"It's not the sea, is it?" asked Mary.

"No, it's miles and miles of wild land on which nothing grows but heather and gorse and broom. The wind blowing through the bushes sounds like the sea."

"I don't like it," Mary said to herself. And she pinched her thin lips together.

They rode through a long, dark group of trees until

they arrived at a large house. The front door was massive, and it opened into an enormous hall. A thin old man, who Mary thought must have been a servant, opened the door for them. "You are to take her to her room," he said to Mrs. Medlock. "He doesn't want to see her. He's going to London in the morning."

Mrs. Medlock led Mary up a large staircase, down a long hallway, and then up another flight of stairs. They went down several more corridors. Finally, she opened a door to a room with a fire in the fireplace and supper on the table.

"Well, here you are," said Mrs. Medlock to Mary. "This room and the next are where you will live—and you must stay in these rooms. Remember that."

It was in this way that Mary Lennox arrived at Misselthwaite Manor. Mary had never felt so sour in all her life.

~ 4 ~

Martha

When Mary awoke in the morning, she found a housemaid lighting a fire in the fireplace. Out of a window she could see a stretch of land with no trees on it that looked like an endless, purplish sea.

"What is that?" she asked, pointing out the window.

Martha, the young housemaid, stood. "That's the moor. Do you like it?"

"No," answered Mary. "I hate it. Do you like it?"

"Aye, I do," said Martha cheerfully. "I love it. It's covered with growing things that smell sweet. It smells of honey, and the birds sing. I wouldn't live away from the moor for anything."

Mary stared at her. The servants in India were not like this. They wouldn't speak unless you spoke to them. They certainly wouldn't talk like this—like a friend.

"You are a strange servant," Mary said in a stiff way.

Martha sat up and laughed. "I know. I talk too much."

"Are you going to be my servant?" asked Mary.

"I'm Mrs. Medlock's servant, and I'll wait on you a

11

bit. But you won't need much waitin' on."

"Who is going to dress me?" Mary asked.

Martha stared, amazed. "You can dress yourself!"

"No. My *ayah* always put on my clothes," Mary said.

"Well, it's time you should learn," said Martha.

"It's different in India," Mary said angrily. "You know nothing about it. You know nothing about anything." And she began to cry, feeling far away from everything she knew.

Martha felt sorry for Mary. "You mustn't cry like that," she said. "I don't know anything—just like you said."

There was something comforting about Martha's Yorkshire accent. Mary stopped crying.

"It's time for you to get up now," said Martha. "I'll help with your clothes if you will get out of bed."

Martha rattled on about her family while Mary was getting dressed. "There are twelve of us children. They tumble about on the moor all day and mother says the air of the moor fattens 'em. Our Dickon, he's twelve years old, finds animals on the moor."

Since she had no *ayah* and had no one to play with, Mary felt lonely. Dickon sounded interesting to her. As she had never been interested in anyone but herself, this was an improvement.

When Mary went to the nursery for breakfast, she found a lot of food on the table. "I don't want it," she said.

"I cannot see good food go to waste," said Martha. "If our children were at this table, they'd clean their plates. They've hardly ever had their stomachs full in their lives."

"I don't know what it is to be hungry," said Mary coldly.

"Well, it would do you good to try it. I can see that."

Mary drank some tea and ate a little toast.

"You wrap up warm and run out and play," said Martha.

"Who will go with me?" Mary asked.

"You'll go by yourself," said Martha. "Our Dickon goes out on the moor and plays by himself for hours."

After hearing about Dickon, Mary decided to go out.

"If you go that way, you'll come to the gardens," Martha said. "One of the gardens has been locked up for ten years."

"Why?" asked Mary.

Martha took a deep breath. "Mr. Craven locked it up and buried the key when his wife died. It was her garden. He won't let anyone inside."

After Mary was outside, she couldn't help thinking of the locked garden. She wondered what it looked like and if anything was still alive in it. She walked through the great gardens. There were bare flowerbeds and a fountain in a large pool. At the end of a long path Mary saw a wall covered with ivy and an open door. Of course, this was not the closed garden.

Just then an old man with a spade walked through the door. He had a crabby face and he did not look happy to see her.

"Can I walk in these gardens?" she asked the man.

"If you like. But there's nothing to see," he said.

So Mary walked on and opened many doors leading into walled gardens. She hoped one of the doors she came to would be locked. Then she would know which garden it was. One of the walled gardens seemed to surround a space inside. She could see the tops of trees in there. Suddenly, a robin sitting on one of the trees burst into song.

The bird looked directly at Mary and sang to her in such a cheerful way. This made her sour face change *almost* into a smile. Mary wondered if the robin lived in the locked garden and knew all about it. She continued walking along the paths.

If Mr. Craven had liked his wife so much, Mary thought, *why did he hate her garden?* She was thinking about the treetop the robin perched on. Then she stopped on the path.

I believe that tree was in the secret garden, Mary thought. *There was a wall around it and there was no door.*

She found the old gardener again, digging in the kitchen garden. "I went into the orchard," she said. "A bird with a red breast sang to me as he was sitting on a tree inside the wall."

To her surprise, a smile crept across the crabby man's face. She had not thought before how much nicer a person looked when he smiled. The man made a soft, low whistle. And the next moment, the robin flew right to him.

"Here he is," chuckled the old man. "I've known

him since he was a fledgling—he was lonely and found me."

Mary took a step toward the robin. "I'm lonely," she said. She did not know that this was one of the things that made her so cross and unpleasant.

"Aren't you the little girl from India?" the man asked.

Mary nodded. "What is your name?"

"Ben Weatherstaff. I'm lonely, too, except when he's with me," he said pointing to the robin. "He's the only friend I've got."

"I have no friends at all," said Mary.

"Then we're a good bit alike," he replied. "We're neither good lookin', and we're both of us as sour as we look."

This was Yorkshire plain speaking, and Mary had never heard the truth about herself. She began to wonder if she was as nasty tempered as Ben Weatherstaff and as unattractive.

The robin flew to a branch near Mary and burst into song again. Ben Weatherstaff laughed out loud.

"He's made up his mind to make friends with you!"

"Would you make friends with me?" she asked the bird in a soft, sweet tone. But after his song, he flew away.

"He's flown over the other wall!" said Mary. "Into the garden without a door."

"He lives there," said old Ben. "He hatched there."

"There must be a door somewhere," she said.

"None that anyone can find," replied Ben. And then he seemed suddenly unhappy with her. "It's none of our business. Don't poke your nose where you shouldn't. I must get to work. You go and play."

Then he stopped digging, threw the spade over his shoulder, and walked off.

~ 5 ~

The Cry in the Corridor

After breakfast, Mary gazed out the window across the huge moor. She knew that if she did not go out she would have to stay inside with nothing to do.

So she went out. She did not know this was the best thing for her. As she ran along the paths, she was getting stronger. The big breaths of fresh air put red color in her cheeks and brightened her dull eyes. Because of her activities outside, Mary awoke one morning knowing what it was to be hungry. She ate until her bowl was empty.

"You go on playin' outdoors every day," Martha said, "and you'll get meat on your bones and you won't be so yellow."

A few days later, Mary saw the robin again. He chirped and hopped along the wall telling her things. Mary laughed and ran after him. "I like you! I like you!" she cried out.

The bird landed on the same tree inside the locked garden.

I wish I could see what's inside, Mary thought. She looked closely at the wall, and still found no door. But there must have been a door if Mr. Craven buried the key to it.

Mary ran along the paths in the fresh air and became more interested in the garden. So much so that she did not feel sorry about coming to Misselthwaite Manor. When she sat down to supper that night, she felt hungry, drowsy, and comfortable. She did not feel cross when Martha chattered away. In fact, she even liked hearing Martha talk.

"Why did Mr. Craven hate the garden?" she asked Martha.

"Mrs. Medlock said it's not to be talked about," she answered. "But I'll tell you a little. Mrs. Craven made the garden when they were first married an' she loved it. She and Mr. Craven used to tend the flowers an' spent hours readin' an' talkin' in the garden. There was an old tree with a branch bent like a seat where she used to sit. But one day, the branch broke an' she fell an' was hurt so bad that she died the next day. That's why he hates it. No one's gone in since, an' he won't let anyone talk about it."

At that moment, Mary felt sorry for Mr. Craven, which was a good thing. In fact, four good things had happened since she came to Misselthwaite. Mary had felt as if she understood a robin and that he understood her; she had run in the wind; she had been healthily hungry for the first time in her life; and she had felt sorry for another person.

While Mary listened to the wind blow around the house, beating at the windows, she also heard something else.

"Do you hear a child crying?" she asked Martha.

Martha suddenly looked confused. "No," she said.

"It's the wind. It can sound like wailing."

"But it sounds as if it's in the house, down a corridor." Just as Mary said this, the wind blew the door open and the crying sound swept down the hall so that it was very clear.

Martha ran and shut the door. But before she did, they both heard the sound of a door banging shut down a hallway.

"It was the wind," said Martha stubbornly. "And if it wasn't, it was little Betty Butterworth, the scullery maid. She had a toothache today."

But the troubled and awkward way Martha said this made Mary believe she was not telling the truth.

There Was Someone Crying

The next day the rain poured down so that Mary could not go out. So she talked with Martha in her room.

"Dickon doesn't mind the wet," Martha said. "He goes out because he sees things on rainy days that you don't on sunny days. He once found a fox cub without a mother in its hole an' brought it home. He found a half-drowned crow another time. Its name is Soot an' it flies with him everywhere."

Mary liked to hear Martha's stories about her family of fourteen people. She most liked stories about Martha's mother and Dickon. It brought a warm, comfortable feeling to Mary when she heard them.

"Well," said Martha, "you could always read somethin'. If Mrs. Medlock lets you go into the library, there are thousands of books there."

Since no one watched over her, Mary decided to go find the library herself. Martha brought her meals every day, but never asked what Mary did. It would be something to do this morning. *Are there really one hundred rooms?* she wondered.

Mary wandered down the corridors with pictures on the walls and found many doors, all closed. She saw a long gallery with portraits covering the walls. She decided to try opening one of the doors. And when she turned the handle, it slowly opened.

Mary found embroidered hangings on the walls and fancy furniture in the room. She opened so many doors after that she lost count and began to get tired. She decided to go back.

Many times Mary lost her way by turning down the wrong corridor. When at last she reached her floor, she didn't know which way to turn. It was very still and quiet. Then the stillness was broken by a sound. It was another cry—a short, childish whine.

Mary put her hand accidentally on the tapestry hanging on the wall. She jumped back in surprise. The tapestry was covering a door, and it fell open. Behind it was a corridor—and Mrs. Medlock was walking toward her with an angry face.

"What are you doing here?" she demanded. "I told you not to wander about." She took Mary's arm and pulled her away.

"I got lost," said Mary. "And I heard someone crying."

"You didn't hear anything," said Mrs. Medlock. "Come back to your nursery right now." And she pulled Mary down the hall. "You stay where you're told to or I'll have to lock you up."

When Mrs. Medlock left, Mary was red with anger. "There *was* someone crying," she said to herself. She had heard it twice now. Mary decided right then to find out who it was.

~ 7 ~

The Key to the Garden

A few days later, Mary sat up in bed and called to Martha. "Look at the moor! Look at the moor!"

The rain had ended, and the gray mist and clouds had gone. A deep blue sky arched over the moor. Never had Mary dreamed of a sky so blue.

"That's because springtime's on its way," said Martha. "I told you that you would like the moor after a bit. Dickon will want to get on the moor at sunrise and stay out all day."

"Could I get there?" asked Mary.

"I don't know," said Martha. "It's five miles to the moor and our cottage. You couldn't walk five miles."

"I would like to see your cottage," said Mary.

Martha looked at Mary. She saw that Mary's face did not look quite as sour. Martha could see that she wanted to go.

"I like your mother," said Mary. "And I like Dickon, even though I've never even seen him. But he wouldn't like me. No one does."

"Well," Martha replied, "how do you like yourself?"

Mary took a breath. "Not at all really. But I never thought of that before."

Martha left to go home to her cottage and help her mother for a day. But Mary felt lonely when she was gone. She went outside and ran around the flower garden ten times. After that, she felt a bit better.

Mary had begun to like the garden as she had begun to like the robin and Dickon and Martha's mother. She was beginning to like Martha, too. That's a good many people to like when you weren't used to liking.

When Mary heard a chirp and a twitter, she looked to her left to see the robin hopping around in a bare flowerbed. The robin had followed her. She bent closer to the bird and he did not back away. Mary forgot she had ever felt sour in her life.

The bird hopped about some more and stopped on a pile of dirt that had been dug up. He was looking for a worm. Mary moved closer and saw a rusty metal ring sticking out of the dirt. She bent to pick it up. It was more than a ring, however. It was an old key that looked like it had been buried for a long time.

Mary stood and held up the key. "Perhaps it has been buried for ten years," she said in a whisper. "Maybe it is the key to the secret garden!"

~ 8 ~

The Robin Showed the Way

Mary looked at the key for a long time. If it was the key to the garden, maybe she could find the door and open it.

She walked along the pathways and looked over the wall at the treetops inside. It seemed silly to be so close to the garden but not be able to get in. She decided she would always keep the key with her so she would be ready if she ever found the door.

In the morning, Martha was back from her family's cottage and served breakfast with rosy cheeks and a bright smile. She said her family enjoyed hearing about the girl from India.

"Mother asked if you had a governess or a nurse," said Martha. "She told me to do my best to cheer you up."

"You do," said Mary.

Martha left the room and came back with something in her apron. "I've brought you a present," she said with a grin.

"A present!" exclaimed Mary. *How could a family of fourteen hungry people give anyone a present?* Mary wondered.

"Mother said nothin' will do you more good than skippin' rope," Martha said. "It will give you strength in your legs."

Martha proudly pulled out a strong, thin rope with striped red and blue handles. Mary had never seen a skipping rope, so Martha had to show her how to use it.

When Mary went to the door to go out, she stopped suddenly. "Martha," she said, "your wages were used to buy the rope. Thank you." She said it stiffly because she was not in the habit of thanking people. "Thank you," she said again.

Once she was outside, Mary skipped and counted until her cheeks were red. She was so excited that when she saw Ben Weatherstaff, she skipped toward him.

"Well," he exclaimed. "You are a young one after all! Maybe you do have blood in your veins instead of sour milk."

Mary skipped around the gardens, resting every few minutes. She went down the long walkway near the locked garden and was so breathless she had to stop. Just then she saw the robin, swaying on a branch of ivy. He had followed Mary.

Mary had heard about magic in her *ayah's* stories, and she always said that what happened next was real magic.

A little gust of wind rushed down the walkway. It was strong enough to blow the sprays of ivy that covered the wall. As the ivy swung aside, Mary saw a round knob. It was the knob of a door.

She pulled the curtain of leaves aside. Her heart was

thumping and her hands were shaking. Mary found a square metal piece with a hole in it. It was the lock of the door that had been closed for ten years.

She put her hand in her pocket and pulled out the key. It fit into the keyhole. It took two hands to turn the key, but it turned.

She took a deep breath and looked up the long walk to see if anyone was coming. The walkway was empty. So she pushed on the heavy door and slowly, slowly it opened.

Mary slipped through the entryway and shut the door behind her. She stood looking around, breathing quickly.

She was standing *inside* the secret garden!

The Strangest House

Inside it was the most wonderful, mysterious place anyone could imagine. The garden walls were covered with leafless stems of climbing roses. And the roses had climbed all over the trees in the garden. It was strange and lovely at the same time.

Mary could not tell if the roses were alive. There were no leaves or flowers on them, and their branches were gray and brown. She hoped that the garden wasn't dead.

"How still everything is!" whispered Mary. "I am the first person who has spoken in here for ten years."

Indeed Mary had found a world all her own.

She decided to skip around the garden and stop to look at things. She came to a place with an old flowerbed. As she bent down, she saw pale green points sticking out of the earth.

"Yes, they are tiny growing things," she whispered. "They might be crocuses or snowdrops or daffodils." Mary looked other places and found more and more green points. "It isn't quite a dead garden," she said excitedly.

She did not know anything about gardening, but

the grass seemed to crowd the green points pushing up. Mary found a sharp piece of wood and knelt down and weeded until there were clear places around the green points.

She decided to do this to all of the green points she could find. She worked in the garden until it was time for her midday meal. When Mary returned to the house, she had bright eyes and red cheeks and ate a great deal.

"Two pieces of meat an' two helpin's of rice puddin'!" Martha said. "Mother will be pleased when I tell her what the skippin' rope did for you!"

Mary thought this was a good time to ask questions. "What are those white roots in the garden that look like onions?"

"They're bulbs," answered Martha. "Lots of spring flowers grow from 'em. Dickon has a whole lot of 'em planted in our garden."

"Does Dickon know about gardening?" asked Mary. She had just thought of a new idea.

"Aye, yes. Dickon can make a flower grow anywhere," said Martha.

"I wish I had a little spade," Mary said.

"What do you want a spade for?" asked Martha.

Mary did not speak right away. She had to be careful not to tell anyone about her secret world. If Mr. Craven found out, he would lock up the garden forever and Mary could not bear that. So she spoke carefully.

"This is a big, lonely place," she began. "If I had a spade, I could dig somewhere and make a little garden."

Martha's face lit up. "Well, if that wasn't just what Mother said! She thought some earth to dig an' plant things in would make you happier. A woman who brings up twelve children knows children."

"How much would a spade cost?" asked Mary. "Mrs. Medlock gives me a shilling a week to spend."

"My word!" said Martha. "That's riches. In the village there's a shop with garden sets for two shillings. I've also seen flower seeds. Dickon knows which are the prettiest. Let's write him a letter and ask him to buy those things for you."

"Oh, that would be wonderful!" exclaimed Mary.

"He'll bring 'em to you himself," said Martha.

"I would like to see the boy whom foxes and crows love!" said Mary.

Mary waited for Martha to return with tea that afternoon. When she came back, Mary looked at Martha carefully. "Has the scullery maid had a toothache today?"

Martha appeared startled. "Why do you ask?" she said.

"I heard the crying again—and there's no wind today."

"You mustn't go walkin' about in the corridors and listenin'," Martha said. "Mr. Craven would be angry. Oh, there's Mrs. Medlock's bell." She almost ran out of the room.

This is a very strange house, thought Mary drowsily. All of the fresh air, skipping rope, and digging had made her tired, and she fell off to sleep.

~ 10 ~

Dickon

The sun shone down on the secret garden for almost a week. Mary loved the feeling that when she was shut inside its walls, no one knew where she was.

Mary was beginning to like being outdoors. Now she could run faster and longer and she could skip rope one hundred times. In the garden, Mary found many more sprouting green points than she had ever hoped to find. Martha had said there had once been "thousands of snowdrops" there.

During the week, Mary spoke to Ben Weatherstaff a bit more. He rarely talked much, but one morning he said more than usual.

"How long have you been here?" he asked Mary.

"About a month," she answered.

"Well, Misselthwaite is doing you good," he said. "You're a bit fatter and not quite so yellow. I'd never seen such an ugly, sour-faced young one when you came."

Mary was not upset by what he said because she knew he was telling the truth.

"If you had your own garden," asked Mary, "what flowers would you plant?"

"Sweet-smellin' things, but mostly roses," he said.

Mary's face brightened. "Do you like roses?"

"Yes," he replied. "I learned from a young lady I was gardener for. She had many and loved 'em like children. That was ten years ago."

"Where is she now?" asked Mary, very interested.

"Heaven," he replied.

"What happened to the roses?" she asked.

"They were left to themselves."

Mary asked as many questions as she dared, and then Ben Weatherstaff looked at her curiously. "Why do you care so much about roses all of a sudden?" he asked.

"I—I want to play that I have a garden of my own," she said. "Do you go and see the roses now?"

"I used to work on them once or twice a year, but I've not been this year. My rheumatism has made me too stiff." He said this in a grumbling voice and then, once again, he suddenly seemed to get angry. "Now look here. You ask more questions than anyone I know. Go play now. I'm done talkin' for today."

Strange as Ben Weatherstaff was, Mary liked him. And he seemed to know everything about the world of flowers.

Mary skipped off and soon heard a peculiar whistling sound. As she turned, she caught her breath. A boy was sitting under a tree playing a wooden pipe. A squirrel watched him closely, and in a bush a pheasant stretched his neck to listen. Two rabbits sat up and looked as if they were coming closer.

When the boy saw Mary, he stopped playing. "I'm Dickon," he said. "I know you are Mary." Dickon had bright blue eyes and a smile that spread across his face.

He bent down and picked up a package. "I've got the garden tools," he said. "There's a spade an' rake an' fork an' hoe. I bought seeds, too."

"Will you show the seeds to me?" Mary asked.

The two sat down to look at the seed packets. Dickon told Mary about each one. Then he stopped and turned his head. "Where's that robin that's callin' us?" he asked. "He's callin' someone he's friends with. Is it you?"

"He likes me a little, I think," said Mary.

"Aye, he does. He's a friend of yours," he said with a smile. Dickon continued to tell Mary how to plant each flower. "I'll plant them for you myself. Where's the garden?"

Mary clutched her hands together and her face turned red. She did not know what to say. She did not think she should tell Dickon about the garden.

"Wouldn't they give you a bit of garden?" Dickon asked carefully. He could see she was upset about something. Mary didn't answer. Then she turned to face Dickon.

"Could you keep a secret?" she asked him slowly. "It's a great secret. I don't know what I'd do if anyone found out. I believe I should die!" she said fiercely.

Dickon looked puzzled. "I'm keepin' secrets all the time," he said. "If I couldn't keep secrets from other boys, secrets about fox cubs and birds' nests, there'd be nothing left on the moor. Aye, I can keep secrets."

Mary put her hand on his sleeve. "I've stolen a garden," she said quickly. "Nobody wants it. Nobody cares for it or goes into it. Perhaps everything is dead.

I don't know." She began to feel stubborn again. "But I don't care! Nobody has any right to take it from me when I care about it. They're letting it die!" she said and threw her arms over her face as she burst into tears.

Dickon's eyes grew wider. "Eh, where is it?" he asked in a soft voice.

Mary lifted her head. "Come with me," she said, "and I'll show you."

She led Dickon down the path and onto the long walkway. When she stopped to lift the curtain of ivy that covered the door, Dickon was so surprised that he jumped a little.

When they were safely inside, Mary waved her arm through the air. "This is it, the secret garden, and I'm the only one in the world who wants it to be alive."

The Nest of the Missel Thrush

For two or three minutes, Dickon stood looking around the garden without saying a word. Mary watched him carefully.

"I never thought I'd see this place," he whispered at last. "Martha told me about it. I wondered what it was like inside."

Dickon walked softly around the garden. "Come springtime this will be the safest nestin' place in England!"

"Will there be roses?" whispered Mary hopefully. "Can you tell? I thought they might all be dead."

"Not all of them—look here." He pushed back some of the branches and showed her a branch that looked brownish green.

"That's as alive as you an' me!" Dickon exclaimed.

Mary almost panted with excitement. "Let's go around the garden and count the ones that are alive!" she said.

They went from tree to bush to tree. Dickon explained that if the dead wood were cut away and the big root dug around, the roses would live. They used

Mary's new spade, hoe, and fork. Then Dickon stopped suddenly.

"Why," he cried. "Who did this?" He was looking at one of Mary's clearings around the green points.

"I did," said Mary quietly. "They looked like they needed to breathe."

"I thought you didn't know nothin' about gardenin'," said Dickon. "A gardener couldn't have done it better. There are crocuses an' snowdrops an' narcissus an' look —daffydowndillys! You've done a lot of work, but there is still a lot to do here."

"Will you help me do it?" asked Mary.

"I'll come every day if you want me," he said with a smile. "It's the best fun I ever had—wakin' up a secret garden."

Mary smiled broadly. Then Dickon looked around again, with a puzzled look this time. "It's a secret garden surely, but there's been a bit of prunin' done—later than ten years ago."

"How?" asked Mary. "The door was locked and the key was buried."

Dickon shook his head. "Aye, how could it?"

The pair worked together side by side for a while and Mary kept looking over at Dickon. "Dickon," she finally said, "you are as nice as Martha said you were. You make the fifth person whom I like."

Dickon sat up. "Only five? Who are the other four?"

"Your mother and Martha." Mary counted on her fingers. "And the robin and Ben Weatherstaff."

Dickon laughed so hard that he felt he should cover his mouth. Then Mary leaned over and asked a question she never had before. She tried in a Yorkshire accent. "Do you like me?"

"Eh!" he answered. "That I do. And so does the robin."

"That's two then," Mary said with a grin.

Soon it was time for Mary to leave for her midday meal. When she got to the garden door, she looked back at Dickon.

"Whatever happens, you'll never tell?" she asked.

"If you were a missel thrush an' showed me your nest, do you think I'd tell anyone?" he said. "You are as safe as a missel thrush."

And she was quite sure she was.

~ 12 ~

"May I Have a Bit of Earth?"

Martha was waiting for Mary when she got to her room.

"I've seen Dickon!" exclaimed Mary. "And I think he's wonderful! His eyes are the same color as the sky on the moor."

Martha chuckled with delight.

"If I found a bit of earth that was out of the way and no one wanted it," asked Mary, "no one would mind me having it, would they?"

"No, there wouldn't be any harm in that," replied Martha.

After Mary ate her meal, Martha told her that Mr. Craven had come back that morning and wanted to see her.

Mary turned pale. "Why? He didn't want to see me when I came."

"Well," said Martha, "Mrs. Medlock said it's because of Mother. She saw Mr. Craven in the village and talked to him about you. Mr. Craven leaves again tomorrow for a long time."

If Mr. Craven didn't return until autumn, Mary

thought, *I will have time to watch the secret garden come alive.*

Mrs. Medlock walked in. "Go and brush your hair, Mary," she said. "And put on your best dress. Mr. Craven will see you in his study."

Mary got ready and followed Mrs. Medlock to a part of the house she had not been in before. The housekeeper knocked on a door. When they entered, she saw a man was sitting in an armchair by the fire.

"This is Mary, sir," said Mrs. Medlock and left.

Mary stood waiting, twisting her hands together. She could see that the man was not a hunchback but had high, crooked shoulders.

"Come here," he said to her gruffly. Mary went to him. He was not ugly. His face would have been handsome if he was not so miserable. Looking at Mary seemed to worry him.

"Do they take good care of you?" he asked.

"Yes," answered Mary quietly.

He rubbed his forehead. "You are very thin."

"I am getting fatter," said Mary in her stiffest way.

Mr. Craven had such an unhappy face. His black eyes hardly seemed to see Mary. "I meant to send you a governess or a nurse, but I forgot," he said.

"I am—" Mary started but a lump in her throat choked her. "I am too big for a nurse."

"That's what Martha's mother, Susan Sowerby, said," he answered. "What do you want to do?"

"I want to play outdoors," said Mary, hoping her voice did not tremble. "I like to skip and look around to see if anything new is sticking out of the earth. I don't do any harm."

"Don't look so frightened," Mr. Craven said. "You won't do any harm and you may do what you like. I wish you to be happy and comfortable. I sent for you because Mrs. Sowerby said that I ought to. I see that she said some sensible things. Play out of doors as much as you'd like and where you like. Is there anything you want? Toys, books, dolls?"

"Might I," started Mary. "Might I have a bit of earth?"

Mr. Craven looked surprised. "Earth?" he asked.

"To plant seeds in—to make things grow—to see them come alive," Mary said.

He looked at Mary for a moment and then looked down.

"Do you care about gardens so much?" he said slowly.

"I didn't in India, but here it is different," she replied.

Mr. Craven got up and walked across the room. He stopped and looked at Mary with soft, kind eyes.

"You can have as much earth as you want," he said. "You remind me of someone else who loved the earth and things that grow. When you see some earth you want, make it come alive!"

Then he appeared sad all of a sudden. "There," he said, "you must go now. I shall be away all summer."

He rang the bell for Mrs. Medlock. "I see what Susan Sowerby was talking about," he said to her. "Give Mary simple, healthy food and let her run wild

39

in the garden. You don't need to look after her too much. Mrs. Sowerby can come and see her now and then and she may sometimes go to the cottage."

"Thank you, sir," Mrs. Medlock said.

Mary flew back to her room and found Martha. "I can have my garden!" she cried. "Your mother is coming to see me and I may go to your cottage! He says I can do what I like—anywhere!"

"Eh," said Martha with a smile, "that was nice of him."

Mary ran as quickly as she could to the garden. She knew Dickon had to leave to walk the five miles home. But when she slipped through the door, she saw he was already gone. A piece of white paper on a rose bush caught her eye. On it was a roughly drawn picture of a bird on a nest—a missel thrush. Then Mary knew Dickon would keep her secret.

~ 13 ~

"I Am Colin"

Mary awakened that night to the rain beating against her window and the wind whirling around noisily. Suddenly she sat upright in bed. "That is not the wind now," she whispered. "That is the crying I heard before."

Mary walked out the door of her room. In the corridor, she could hear the far-off crying more clearly. She felt that she must find out what it was. It was even more mysterious to her than the locked garden.

Mary held the candle from her bedside to light the way. The corridor was long and dark, but she found the door covered with the tapestry. Once inside the hallway, she saw a sliver of light shone from a door down the hall.

Mary walked to the door and pushed it open. She stood in a room with handsome furniture, a fireplace, and a four-poster bed. On the bed was a boy, crying.

The boy had a pale face and very big eyes, too big for his face. He looked ill, but he seemed to be crying as if he was tired and not because he was in pain. As Mary came closer, the boy stared at her with wide eyes.

"Who are you?" he asked in a whisper. "Are you a ghost?"

"No," said Mary. "Are you?"

"No, I am Colin Craven. Who are you?"

"I am Mary Lennox. Mr. Craven is my uncle."

"He is my father," the boy said.

"Your father?" Mary gasped. "No one told me about you! Did you know about me?"

"No," said Colin. "They wouldn't tell me because I would be afraid you would see me. I am always ill. My father won't allow the servants to talk about me. If I live, I will be a hunchback. But I won't live. I've heard people say it when they think I'm not listening."

"What a strange house this is!" cried Mary. "There are so many secrets. Does your father come see you?"

"Sometimes," Colin answered. "Usually when I am asleep. My mother died when I was born and he feels terrible when he sees me. I think he hates me."

"He hates the garden because she died," Mary said quietly.

"What garden?" Colin asked.

"A garden she liked," she said quickly. "Have you always been here?" Mary wanted to change the subject.

"Nearly," he said. "I don't like to go out in the fresh air."

"I didn't either, when I first came," Mary said. Then a thought crept into her mind. "If you don't want people to see you, do you want me to go away?"

"No," he said. "I want to hear about you."

So Mary sat down. She told Colin about India and

her time at Misselthwaite. Mary learned that Colin could have whatever he wanted and he seemed a spoiled child. "It makes me sick to be angry," he said. "So everyone does what I like."

Colin asked Mary how old she was. When Mary answered, she forgot herself. "I am ten," she said, "and so are you."

"How do you know that?"

"Because when you were born," she said, "the garden door was locked and the key was buried. It has been ten years."

"What garden door?" he asked with interest. "Who did it?"

"It is the garden Mr. Craven hates," Mary said nervously. It was too late to be careful. "He locked the door and no one knows where he buried the key. No one will talk about it."

Colin had little to do or think about alone in his room all day. The idea of a hidden garden was exciting. "I want to see that garden more than anything else," he said. "I want the door unlocked. I will make them take me there in my chair."

Mary clasped her hands together. Everything would be spoiled! Dickon would never come back. She would never feel like a bird in a safe nest again. "Oh, don't— don't do that! Please don't!" she cried out.

Colin stared at Mary as if she had gone crazy. "Why?"

"If you make them open the door, it will never be a secret again," Mary answered. "But if we find the hidden door, it could be our garden—our secret and no one would know we were in it. We could be there every day and make it come alive.

"I'm sure we could find the door," Mary went on. "Maybe we could get a boy to push you and we could go there alone."

"I would like that," said Colin, his eyes looking dreamy. Then he turned to Mary. "I want you to see something," he said. "Pull the curtain cord that's hanging over the mantel."

When the curtains parted, a painting of a girl with a happy, laughing face was there. She had lovely gray eyes just like Colin.

"She is my mother," he said. "I don't know why she died. If she had lived, I don't think I would be ill. And my father would not hate to look at me. Close the curtain again."

Mary did as she was told. "Why is she covered up?"

"Sometimes I don't like her looking at me," he said. "She smiles too much when I am unhappy."

Colin glanced at Mary. "Will you come here every day?"

"I will come as often as I can," she replied. "But I still have to look for the garden door every day."

"Yes, you must," said Colin. "And you can come and tell me about it. I think you will be a secret, too. Martha can tell you when to come—when my nurse is out. Do you know Martha?"

"Yes," said Mary. "She waits on me."

Then Mary understood Martha's worried look when she asked about the crying. Martha had known about Colin all along and she wasn't supposed to tell anyone about him.

"I wish I could go to sleep before you leave," Colin said.

"I can sing to you like my *ayah* used to sing to me," offered Mary. Then she sang a low chanting song in Hindustani.

Soon Colin was fast asleep.

~ 14 ~

The Visit

When Martha arrived the next morning, she knew at once that Mary had something to tell her.

"I have found out what the crying was," said Mary. "I found Colin."

Martha's face paled. "Eh! If Mrs. Medlock finds out, she'll think I disobeyed orders and told you about him!"

"Colin is not going to tell Mrs. Medlock yet," said Mary. "And he was glad I came. We talked for a long time. Before I left, I sang him to sleep."

Martha gasped in amazement. "I can scarcely believe you!"

"He wants you to bring me to him every day," said Mary. "And what is the matter with him?"

"No one is sure," said Martha. "When he was born, his mother died. Mr. Craven went crazy and wouldn't see him. He thought the baby would be another hunchback like him."

"But Colin doesn't look like a hunchback," Mary said.

"He isn't yet," said Martha. "But they are afraid his back is weak. They don't let him walk and they make him lie down. One doctor from London said there had been too much medicine and too much letting him have his own way."

"I think he's a spoiled boy," said Mary.

"The worst there ever was," said Martha.

"Do you think he will die?" asked Mary.

"Mother said there's no reason why a child who gets no fresh air and lies on his back all day should live."

Then a bell rang for Martha and she left the room. A few moments later, Martha came back with a puzzled expression.

"You have worked magic, Miss Mary," she said. "Colin wants to see you."

Martha brought Mary to Colin. When she left, Mary told Colin about Dickon. "Martha's brother is not like anyone else. He can charm foxes and squirrels and birds. He plays a pipe and animals come listen."

Colin's eyes grew larger. "Tell me more about him."

"He knows all about eggs and nests," Mary went on. "He knows everything that grows or lives on the moor."

"You never get to see anything if you are ill," said Colin.

"Not if you stay in your room," said Mary.

"I can't go on the moor," said Colin in a bitter tone. "I am going to die."

"How do you know?" Mary asked without sympathy.

"I've heard it ever since I can remember," he replied.

"Did the doctor from London say you were going to die?" asked Mary.

"No. He said, 'The lad might live if he would make up his mind to.'"

Mary pulled her stool closer to Colin. "Let's not talk about dying. I don't like it. Let's talk about living."

Mary didn't know it, but it was the best thing she could have said. They talked about Dickon and his mother and brothers and sisters. And they both began to laugh like children do when they are happy together.

In the midst of this laughter, the door opened and in walked the doctor and Mrs. Medlock. The doctor jumped in actual alarm, and Mrs. Medlock almost fell backwards.

"Goodness!" exclaimed Mrs. Medlock.

"What is this?" said the doctor.

"This is my cousin, Mary Lennox," said Colin calmly. "I asked her to come. She must come whenever I send for her."

The doctor looked at Mrs. Medlock as if she were to blame.

"Nobody told Mary anything," explained Colin. "She found me herself."

Mary saw that the doctor did not look pleased as he reached for Colin's wrist to take his pulse.

"There has been too much excitement," he said.

"I shall become too excited if Mary is kept away," responded Colin.

Before he left, the doctor gave his words of warning. Colin must not talk too much. He must not forget that he is ill. He must not forget that he gets tired easily. Mary thought that was a lot of uncomfortable things he was not to forget.

"But I want to forget," Colin replied. "She makes me forget. That is why I want her here."

Nest Building

A week of rain followed before the sun came up. Mary enjoyed herself, though, because she had spent every day with Colin. They talked about gardens and Dickon and his cottage.

"You are sly to get out of your bed and wander around," Mrs. Medlock said to Mary. "But it's been a blessing to us. Colin has not had a tantrum since you made friends."

In her talks with Colin, Mary was careful not to tell him that she had found the secret garden. She wanted to find out first if he could keep a secret. If he could be trusted, Mary wondered if she could take Colin there without anyone finding out.

She thought that if Colin saw the animals and the garden, he might not think so much about dying. Mary had seen herself in the mirror lately and she realized she looked quite different than when she arrived from India. The child she saw in the mirror looked kinder, and even happier.

If the gardens and fresh air had been good for her, maybe they would be good for Colin. But if he hated people to look at him, maybe he would not want Dickon to see him.

"People used to stare at me when I went out,"

Colin said. "They would whisper and I knew they were saying I wouldn't live to grow up."

"Would you hate it if a boy looked at you?" Mary asked.

"There's one boy I wouldn't mind," he replied. "Your friend, Dickon. He's a sort of animal charmer and I am a boy animal." They both laughed about that.

On the first morning the sky was blue again and the sun was warm, Mary could not wait to see the garden. She dressed quickly and went outside.

After the week of rain, the grass was greener, things were sticking up everywhere, and leaves were uncurling. She was sure Dickon would come today. When Mary passed through the door of the secret garden, she saw a large crow and a fox cub watching a boy digging.

"Oh, Dickon!" she exclaimed. "You are here and the sun has only just come up!"

"How could I have stayed in bed?" he said. "The world's hummin' an' breathin' an' buildin' today. I ran like mad to get here. The garden was waitin'!"

"I am so happy I can hardly breathe!" said Mary.

Dickon pointed to the fox cub. "It's named Captain. An' the crow is Soot. They both felt same as I did today."

Dickon walked around and Soot stayed on his shoulder while Captain trotted next to him. He showed her leaf buds on rose branches that had seemed dead. They found new green points in the dirt.

When Ben Weatherstaff's robin flew across the wall with something in its beak, Dickon stood still.

"He's buildin' a nest," he whispered. "He'll stay if

we don't scare him." They sat very still. Then Mary spoke quietly.

"Do you know about Colin?" she asked.

Dickon turned his head to look at her. "What do you know about him?"

"I've seen him," she said. "I've talked to him every day this week."

Dickon looked relieved. "I'm glad of that. I knew I must not say nothin' about him."

"How did you know about Colin?" asked Mary.

"Everybody knows. Martha was worried last time she came home. She didn't know what to say when you heard Colin cryin' and started asking questions."

Mary told Dickon how she had found Colin in the night. She described his small pale face and his black-rimmed eyes.

"They're just like his mother's eyes, only hers were always laughin'," Dickon said. "They say Mr. Craven can't bear to see him when he's awake because his eyes are so like hers."

"Colin's so afraid of having a hunchback that he won't sit up," said Mary. "He thinks if he should feel a lump coming he would go crazy and scream himself to death."

"Eh! No lad would get well thinkin' like that," he said.

They watched the fox play on the grass nearby. Then Dickon looked at Mary. "I was thinkin' that if Colin were out here he wouldn't be waitin' for lumps to grow on his back. Do you think we could get him here?"

"I've been wondering that myself," Mary said. "If Colin wants to come out, no one would disobey him. He could order the gardeners to keep away so no one would see us."

"We'll have him here for sure," said Dickon. "The robin and his mate have been buildin' a nest while we've been here."

Mary saw the twig in the robin's beak. Dickon spoke gently to him. "We're nest buildin', too. Don't tell."

~ 16 ~

"I Won't!"

When Mary returned to the house, she still had much to do in the garden. "Tell Colin I can't come and see him yet," she said to Martha.

Martha looked frightened. "Eh! Miss Mary," she said. "It may upset him if I tell him that."

But Mary was not afraid of Colin as other people were. "I can't stay," she said. "Dickon is waiting for me."

That afternoon Mary and Dickon did quite a bit of work in the garden. When it was time to leave, both agreed to return at sunrise.

Mary ran back to the house as quickly as she could. She had so much to tell Colin. But when she opened the door of her room, she found Martha waiting for her with an unhappy face.

"I wish you had gone to him," she said. "He's almost goin' into one of his tantrums."

Colin was lying flat on his back in bed when Mary arrived. He did not turn his head when she marched up to him.

"Why didn't you get out of bed today?" she asked.

"I made them put me in bed when you didn't come.

My back ached and my head hurt. Why didn't you come?"

"I was working in the garden with Dickon," said Mary.

Colin frowned. "I won't let that boy come here if you go and stay with him instead of coming to see me," he said.

Mary was furious. "If you send Dickon away, I won't come into this room again!"

"I'll make you," said Colin.

"They can drag me in," said Mary, "but they can't make me talk to you!"

The two angry children glared at each other. "You are a very selfish thing!" cried Colin.

"You're the most selfish boy I ever saw!" yelled Mary.

"I am not as selfish as your Dickon!" Colin snapped. "He keeps playing in the dirt when he knows I am all by myself."

Mary's eyes flashed fire. "He's nicer than any other boy that ever lived!" she said.

Colin turned his head on his pillow and a tear slid down his face. "I'm not as selfish as you because I am ill. I am sure I feel a lump coming on my back and I am going to die."

"You are not!" said Mary.

Colin opened his eyes wide. He had never heard such a thing said before. "I'm not? You know I am! Everybody says so."

"I don't believe it!" Mary said sourly.

In spite of his weak back, Colin sat up in bed. "Get

out!" he shouted. Then he grabbed his pillow and threw it at her.

"I'm going," replied Mary. "And I won't come back! I was going to tell you all sorts of nice things. Now I won't!"

She marched out of the room. To Mary's surprise, the nurse was standing outside the door listening. And she was laughing.

"The best thing to happen to that spoiled boy," the nurse giggled, "is to have someone stand up to him who's as spoiled as he."

"Is he going to die?" asked Mary, rather annoyed.

"I don't know and I don't care," replied the nurse. "Hysterics and temper are half of what makes him sick."

Mary was cross and disappointed, but she was not sorry for Colin. She had thought she could trust him with her secret, but now she had changed her mind. She would never tell him.

When Mary returned to her room, Martha said she had received a box from Mr. Craven. There were games and several beautiful books about gardens. Slowly her anger began to fade. Mary had not expected Mr. Craven to remember her, and it warmed her heart.

She looked at the gifts and thought about Colin. Mary knew that Colin worried about his back when he was angry or frightened. He was certainly angry now. And she knew his tantrums usually started when he worried.

I said I would never go back, thought Mary, *but perhaps I will go see him in the morning.*

17

A Tantrum

Mary awoke late that night to dreadful sounds. Doors were opening and closing and she heard footsteps hurrying in the corridors. Someone was screaming in a horrible way.

It's Colin, thought Mary. *He's having one of those tantrums.* She put her hands over her ears and felt sick and shivery. *I can't bear it,* she thought. Mary was so frightened by the sound that she became angry.

Then the nurse came in. "He's worked himself into hysterics and he'll do himself harm," she said. "No one can do anything. You come and try."

The closer Mary got to the screams, the angrier she became. She slapped Colin's door open with her hand and ran across the room to his bed.

"You stop!" she shouted. "I wish everybody would run out of the house and let you scream yourself to death!" The shock of those nasty words was the best thing for this hysterical boy. He almost jumped at the sound of Mary's furious little voice.

Colin's face looked dreadful, but Mary did not care. "If you scream another scream," she said, "I'll scream too—and I can scream louder than you can."

"I can't stop," Colin gasped and sobbed.

"You can!" shouted Mary. "Half the reason you are sick is from hysterics and temper."

"I felt the lump," choked Colin. "I felt it. I shall have a hunch on my back and then I shall die." He sobbed again.

"You didn't feel a lump!" said Mary fiercely. "There's nothing the matter with your back. Nurse, come show me his back this minute!"

The nurse, Mrs. Medlock, and Martha had been huddled in the corner with their mouths open. The nurse came and lifted Colin's shirt. It was a poor, thin back with every rib showing. Mary bent over and examined his back carefully. The room fell silent.

"There's not a single lump there!" she said at last. "Not one as big as a pin. If you ever say there is again, I shall laugh!"

No one but Colin knew the power of those crossly spoken words. He had never told anyone but Mary his secret fear.

"I didn't know he thought he had a lump on his spine," said the nurse. "His back is weak because he won't try to sit up."

"There!" said Mary.

Colin gulped and turned to Mary. Huge tears streamed down his face and wet the pillow. They were tears of relief.

"Do you think—I could—live to grow up?" he asked the nurse.

"You probably will if you do not give in to your temper and if you stay out in the fresh air," she said.

Colin was weak from his tantrum, but he put out

his hand to Mary. She met Colin's hand with hers. It was their way of making up.

"I'll go outside with you, Mary," said Colin. "And Dickon can come and push my chair."

Mary told the nurse that she would sit with Colin until he fell asleep. When the nurse was gone, Colin asked, "Have you found anything out about the secret garden?"

Mary looked at his weary, swollen face. "Yes," she said, "I think I have. If you go to sleep, I will tell you tomorrow."

Colin's hand trembled. "Oh, Mary!" he said. "If I could get into the secret garden, I think I should live to grow up!"

Then in a low, soothing voice, Mary described to Colin what she said she imagined was inside the secret garden—the climbing roses, the green shoots, and the nesting birds.

Colin could hardly wait until morning.

18

"We Mustn't Waste Any Time"

Colin was quiet and feverish as usual the day after a tantrum. At breakfast, Martha said that Colin was asking for Mary. "And he said 'please.' Think of that!" Martha said with a chuckle. "You did give it to him last night. Nobody else would have dared to."

When Mary entered Colin's room, he was in bed. He looked pale with dark circles under his eyes. "I'm glad you came," he said.

Mary smiled. "I'm going to Dickon," Mary said, "but I won't be long. Colin—it's something about the garden."

"Oh, is it?" he cried. His entire face brightened. "I'll lie and think about it until you come back."

Mary met Dickon in the garden. This morning he brought two squirrels with him, Nut and Shell. When Mary told Dickon about Colin's tantrum, she could see he felt sorrier for Colin than she did. "Poor lad seein' so little that he gets to thinkin' of things that get him screamin'," said Dickon. "Eh! We must get him out here. An' we mustn't waste any time."

"I'll ask if you can come see him tomorrow morning with the creatures," Mary suggested. "Then later, we'll take him out and you can push him in his chair. We'll show him everything." And so it was decided.

Mary went back to the house to see Colin. "What is it you smell of?" he asked. "You smell like flowers and fresh things."

"It comes from the springtime an' sunshine," said Mary in a Yorkshire accent. Colin began to laugh when he heard her speak. They both laughed until they could not stop themselves.

Mrs. Medlock opened the door of Colin's room and stepped back into the corridor. She stood listening, amazed. "Well, my word!" she said. "Who would have thought!"

Mary told Colin about all of the animals Dickon had made friends with. Colin lay quietly for a few moments. "I wish I was friends with things," he said. "But I'm not. I never had anything to be friends with and I can't bear people."

"Can't you bear me?" Mary asked.

"Yes, and I even like you," he replied.

"Ben Weatherstaff said I was like him," said Mary. "He thinks we have the same nasty tempers. I think you are like him, too. I don't feel as sour as I used to, though."

"Mary," Colin said, "I wish I hadn't said what I did about sending Dickon away. And I wouldn't mind Dickon looking at me. I do want to see him."

"I'm glad you said that," said Mary. "Because—"

Suddenly Mary knew this was the minute to tell Colin about the garden.

"Because what?" he asked eagerly.

Mary was so nervous that she got up and held his hands in hers. "Can I trust you?" she asked. "Can I trust you for sure?"

He almost whispered his answer. "Yes—yes!"

"Well, Dickon will come see you tomorrow and he'll bring his creatures with him."

"Oh!" Colin cried out in delight.

"But that's not all," Mary continued. "Here's the best part: I found a door into the garden. It is under the ivy on the wall."

Colin's eyes got bigger and then he gasped for breath. "Oh, Mary!" he cried with a half sob. "Shall I see it? Shall I live to get into it?" He clutched her hands.

"Of course you'll live to get into it!" Mary said.

And just minutes later, Mary was telling Colin not what she imagined the secret garden to be like, but what it really was.

19

"It Has Come!"

As usual, after Colin's tantrum, the doctor was sent for. He had always found a pale, shaken boy lying in bed thereafter. Of course, he expected the same this morning.

"How is he?" he asked Mrs. Medlock.

"Well, sir," she replied, "you'll scarcely believe your eyes. That sour-faced girl has done what none of us dare to do. She ordered him to stop screaming. Come see."

The scene the doctor saw when he entered Colin's room was indeed surprising. Colin was on his sofa sitting up straight and looking at a garden book while he talked to Mary.

The children stopped talking when they saw the doctor.

"I'm sorry to hear you were ill last night," he said.

"I'm better now," Colin replied. "Much better. I'm going out in my chair in a day or so. I want some fresh air."

"I thought you did not like fresh air," the doctor said while taking Colin's pulse.

"I don't when I'm by myself," said Colin, "but Mary is going with me. I will not have a nurse, either. I will have a strong boy push my carriage."

The doctor was alarmed. "He must be a strong boy,

and steady," he said. "Who is he?"

"It's Dickon," Mary spoke suddenly. She saw that the doctor's serious face relaxed at once and broke into a smile.

"Oh, Dickon," the doctor said. "He's as strong as a moor pony. You will be safe enough. Colin, you are evidently better today, but you must remember—"

"I don't want to remember," interrupted Colin. "It is because Mary makes me forget that she makes me better."

The doctor had never had such a short stay after a tantrum. He was very puzzled by what he saw that day.

That night Colin slept without waking, and in the morning he awoke with a smile on his face. His mind was full of plans he and Mary had made yesterday. Then he heard feet running down the hallway. Mary burst into the room.

"It has come!" Mary said breathlessly. "The spring has come!"

"Has it?" cried Colin. He actually sat up in bed. "Open the window!"

Mary opened it wide and told Colin to take deep breaths of the fresh air. "Dickon says he can feel it in his veins and he feels he could live forever and ever."

Colin drew in deep breaths until he felt something delightful was happening to him.

"There are things crowding up out of the earth," said Mary. "There are flowers uncurling, and a green veil has covered the gray branches. The seeds we planted are up and Dickon has brought the fox and the crow and the squirrels and a new lamb."

When the nurse arrived with breakfast, Colin announced to her, "A boy, and a fox, and a crow, and two squirrels, and a newborn lamb are coming to see me this morning. I want them brought up right away."

The nurse gave a slight gasp and said, "Yes, sir."

Mary and Colin talked while they ate a good breakfast. Then Mary said suddenly, "Do you hear a caw? That's Soot."

"Oh, yes!" cried Colin. "They're coming!"

They heard marching footsteps until Martha entered and announced, "If you please, sir, here's Dickon an' his creatures."

Dickon came in smiling his widest smile. The newborn lamb was in his arms and the little red fox trotted by his side. Nut sat on his left shoulder and Soot on his right and Shell's head peeped out of his coat pocket.

Colin stared and stared. He had never talked to a boy in his life and he was so overwhelmed with curiosity that he did not even think of speaking.

Dickon walked over to Colin and put the lamb quietly in his lap. Then he brought a bottle out of his pocket and let the lamb drink noisily from it.

By the time the lamb fell asleep, Colin poured out questions to Dickon and Dickon answered them all. They looked at pictures in the gardening books. Dickon knew all the flowers and which ones were growing in the secret garden.

"I'm going to see them!" cried Colin.

"Yes, you must," said Mary. "And we mustn't waste any time."

20

"I Shall Live Forever"

However, because of bad weather, the children did not go to the garden for a week. But every day Dickon came to see Colin and told him what was happening on the moor.

Preparations were being made to take Colin to the garden in secret. Colin had decided that the mystery about the hidden garden was one of its greatest charms. Nothing should spoil that. So, Colin told the head gardener that he would be going out in his chair and that no one should come near him.

A little while later, the nurse made Colin ready. She noticed that instead of lying like a log while his clothes were put on, he sat up and tried to help himself.

The strongest footman in the house carried Colin downstairs and put him in his wheelchair outside. Dickon began to push the chair slowly and steadily. Mary walked beside it, and Colin leaned back, lifting his face to the sky.

They walked around the shrubbery and fountain beds until they turned into the long walk by the ivied walls.

"This is it," breathed Mary in a whisper.

"Is it?" exclaimed Colin. "But I see no door."

"That's what I thought," said Mary. A few yards later, Mary stopped. "But here is the handle," she said, "and the door. Dickon, push him in—push him in quickly!"

With one strong push, Dickon pushed the chair through the doorway.

Colin had covered his eyes with his hands until they were inside and the door was closed. When he took them away, he looked around and around the garden just as Mary and Dickon had done. He saw the green veil of leaves creeping over walls and earth. In the grass and under the trees were splashes of gold and purple and white flowers. He heard the fluttering of wings and smelled the scents of things growing.

In wonder, Mary and Dickon stared at Colin. He looked so strange and different because a pink glow of color had crept all over him—over his ivory face and neck and all.

"I shall get well!" Colin cried out. "Mary, Dickon, I shall get well! And I shall live forever and ever!"

21

Ben Weatherstaff

When Colin first saw the springtime in the hidden garden, it seemed that the whole world wanted to show its beauty to one boy. They put Colin's chair under the plum tree, which was snow-white with blossoms and musical with bees.

Mary and Dickon worked in the garden as Colin watched them. "I wonder if we shall see the robin," said Colin. Then he saw something he had not noticed before. "That's a very old tree there, isn't it?"

Dickon and Mary looked across the grass at the tree and were quiet. "Yes," answered Dickon in a low, gentle voice.

"The branches are quite gray," Colin went on. "And it looks as if a branch has broken off. I wonder how it was done."

"It's been many a year," said Dickon.

Suddenly, Dickon saw the robin. "Eh! There he is! He's been finding food for his mate!"

Colin leaned back on his cushion laughing a little. "He's taking tea to her," he said.

And so they were safe for the moment.

"Magic sent the robin," Mary said later to Dickon. "We could never tell him how the tree broke, poor lad," said Dickon. "Mrs. Craven was a lovely young lady. Mother thinks she's at Misselthwaite lookin' after Master Colin sometimes. Maybe she's been in the garden an' maybe she told us to bring Colin here."

A few moments later, Colin looked around him and sighed. "I don't want the afternoon to end. But I will come back tomorrow and the next day and the next. I'm going to see everything grow here. I'm going to grow here myself."

"That you will," said Dickon with a smile. "We'll have you walkin' an' diggin' same as other folk."

"Walk!" said Colin excitedly. "Dig! Shall I?"

"For sure you will," Dickon said firmly.

"Nothing really ails my legs," Colin said. "They are weak and they shake so much I am afraid to stand on them."

"When you stop being afraid," said Dickon, "you will stand on 'em."

Colin lay still and thought about all of this. Then he lifted his head and said in a loud whisper. "Who is that man?"

Dickon and Mary scrambled to their feet. Colin pointed at the high wall. "There!" he said.

Mary and Dickon turned around. There was Ben Weatherstaff looking at them over the wall. He stood frozen in amazement and curiosity. "However did you get in?" he said.

"It was the robin that showed me the way," said Mary. "He didn't know he did it, but he did."

Ben stared hard at something behind Mary.

"Wheel me over there," said Colin to Dickon.

The sight of Colin coming across the grass made Ben Weatherstaff's jaw drop.

"Do you know who I am?" asked Colin.

Ben gulped down a lump in his throat and could not say a word. Then he replied in shaky voice. "Aye, that I do—with your mother's eyes starin' at me. Lord knows how you came here. You are the poor cripple."

"I am not!" cried Colin furiously.

"You haven't got a crooked back?" Ben asked with a hoarse voice, "or crooked legs?"

"No!" Colin said. Now the strength with which he usually threw his tantrums rushed through his body. He had never been accused of having crooked legs, even in whispers. His anger and insulted pride filled him with a power he had never known.

"Come here!" Colin shouted to Dickon. Dickon ran to his side and Mary let out a short gasp. "He can do it! He can do it!" she whispered under her breath.

Colin tossed the blankets from his legs onto the ground. Dickon held his arm and Colin's thin legs were out and on the grass in seconds. Then Colin was standing upright—upright, straight, and tall. His head was thrown back and his eyes flashed like lightning.

"Look at me!" he shouted to Ben.

"He is as straight as I am!" cried Dickon. "He's as straight as any lad in Yorkshire!"

What Ben Weatherstaff did next was strange indeed. He choked and gulped and suddenly tears ran down his wrinkled cheeks. "Eh!" he burst out. "The lies folks tell! You will be a man yet. God bless you!"

Colin continued to stand up straight. "This is my

garden," he said. "Come down and Mary will bring you in here. I want to talk to you. Now you will have to be in on the secret. Be quick!"

Ben seemed unable to take his eyes off Colin. "Yes, sir!" he said as he climbed down the ladder.

~ 22 ~

When the Sun Went Down

Dickon watched Colin with sharp eyes while Mary went to meet Ben on the walkway. "I've stopped being afraid," said Colin. "And I'm going to walk to that tree." With help from Dickon, he did just that.

When Ben Weatherstaff came through the door, he saw Colin standing. Mary whispered to herself, "You can do it!"

"What have you been doin' with yourself, letting people think you were a cripple?" Ben asked.

"Everyone thought I was going to die," said Colin. "And I'm not."

Ben looked him up and down and said, "Nothing of the sort! When I saw you put your legs on the ground in such a hurry, I knew you were all right. Sit down, young master, and give me your orders."

There was tenderness and understanding in Ben's voice. Mary had talked to him as fast as she could when they walked toward the garden. She had told him to remember that Colin was getting well—*getting* well. The garden was doing it. No one must let him think of lumps and dying.

"What work do you do in the gardens?" asked Colin.

"Anything I'm told to do," replied Ben. "I'm kept on here because she liked me."

"She?" asked Colin.

"Your mother," he replied. "This was her garden. She was very fond of it."

"It is my garden now," said Colin, "and I am fond of it. But it is a secret. My orders are that no one knows we come here. I will send for you to help, but come only when no one will know."

"I've come when no one knows," Ben Weatherstaff said with a smile. "The last time I was here was about two years ago. But my rheumatism has held me back since then."

"You came an' did a bit o' prunin'!" cried Dickon. "I couldn't figure out how it had been done."

"Your mother was so fond of the garden," Ben said. "'Ben,' she had said laughin', 'if I'm ever ill or I go away, you must take care of my roses.' When she did go away, the orders were that no one should come here. But I came," he said stubbornly. "She gave her orders first."

"I'm glad you did," said Colin.

Colin picked up a trowel on the grass and scratched at the earth with his thin, weak hand. He kept going and soon he had dug a small hole.

Colin spoke to Dickon in a Yorkshire accent. "You said I'd be walkin' about an' diggin' same as other folk. This is only the first day an' I've walked—an' here I am diggin'."

Ben Weatherstaff's mouth fell open when he heard

Colin speak in a Yorkshire accent. Now he chuckled. "You are a Yorkshire lad for sure. How'd you like to plant somethin'?"

Ben left and he returned with a rose plant. "Here, lad, set it in the earth yourself."

Colin's weak, white hands shook a little when he put the rose in the hole, but he did it. "It's planted!" he said. "Now help me up, Dickon."

And when the sun went down that day, Colin was standing on his own two feet—and laughing.

~ 23 ~

Magic

Colin's doctor had been waiting a long time when the children returned to the house. "You should not have stayed so long," he said to Colin.

"I am not tired at all," he replied. "Tomorrow I am going out in the morning as well as the afternoon."

"I do not think I can allow it," answered the doctor.

"It would not be wise to stop me," said Colin.

Mary had once been as stubborn and rude as Colin. But since she had been at Misselthwaite, she had learned that her rudeness was not popular with others.

"I am sorry for the doctor," said Mary. "It must be quite horrible to have to be polite to a ten-year-old boy who is rude."

"Am I rude?" asked Colin.

"Yes," said Mary. "Nobody ever dared do anything you wouldn't like—because you were a poor thing who might die."

"But I'm not," said Colin stubbornly. "I stood on my feet this afternoon."

"Because you have always gotten your own way, you are a bit strange and so am I. But I was much stranger before I began to like people and before I found the garden."

"I don't want to be strange," said Colin. "I will stop being so if I go to the garden every day. I think there is magic there."

They always called it magic. And indeed it seemed to be magic that made everything change in the months that followed. The seeds Dickon and Mary planted grew as if fairies had tended them. And the roses tangling the trees and spreading over the walls came alive hour by hour.

Colin saw it all. He spent every day that it didn't rain in the garden. He talked of magic and Mary told him how she had whispered encouragement under her breath on the day he first walked.

"I am going to try an experiment," Colin announced one day. He asked Mary and Dickon and Ben Weatherstaff to stand in front of him. "When I grow up I am going to make great scientific discoveries. This shall be the first one.

"The magic in this garden has made me stand up and know that I will live to be a man," Colin said. "My experiment will be to say 'The magic is in me! The magic is making me well!' every day. Perhaps it will make me well. You all can help me do this."

"We will," all three replied.

"Do you think it will work?" Colin asked Dickon.

"Aye," he answered. "I do."

And then Colin announced, "Now I am going to walk around the garden." And they all went with him. Colin was at the head of the line with Mary and Dickon at his sides. Ben Weatherstaff followed and the creatures fell in line behind him.

"The magic is in me! I can feel it," Colin chanted. He would stop and rest and lean on Dickon. But he did not give up until he had walked all the way around the garden. When he returned to the tree, his cheeks were pink. "I did it!" he cried.

"What will the doctor say?" Mary asked.

"He won't say anything," said Colin, "because he will not be told. This is to be the biggest secret of all. No one is to know until I have grown so strong that I can run like any other boy. I will come here every day in my chair and I shall go back in it. When my father comes back, I shall walk into his study and say, 'I am well and I shall live to be a man.'"

~ 24 ~

"Let Them Laugh"

In the evening hours, Dickon would tell his mother about his day. Soon they decided that she could also keep the secret.

"My word!" Mrs. Sowerby said when she heard the whole story. "It's a good thing that little girl came to Misselthwaite. It's been the makin' of her and the savin' of him."

"Every day, Colin's face looks rounder and not as waxy," said Dickon. "But he keeps complainin', so no one guesses he's getting better. Mary and Colin have to do some playactin'. Outside, Colin never lifts his head up until we're out of sight. When we are safe inside the garden, they laugh and laugh."

"Laughin's better than pills any day," Mrs. Sowerby replied.

Dickon told his mother about Colin's visit from the doctor and nurse that day.

"I don't think being out all day has done you harm," the doctor had said. "The nurse says you eat more than ever before."

"Perhaps it is an unnatural appetite," said Colin. "Perhaps I am bloated and feverish."

"I don't think so," the doctor replied. "If you keep

this up, we need not talk of dying. Your father will be happy about this."

"He is not to be told!" cried Colin. "If I get worse, he will be disappointed. I won't have letters written to my father!"

"Nothing shall be written without your permission," the doctor answered.

For the time being, it seemed that Colin's playacting was working. The children had made up their minds to eat less, but it was hard to do when they awoke each morning with huge, healthy appetites.

Every day now Colin chanted about the magic and took his walk around the garden. He became stronger and stronger. The children learned exercises to build their muscles, too.

"They are eating less," said the nurse to the doctor. "And yet see how plump they are getting."

"Well," he said, "as long as going without food agrees with him, we need not worry. The boy is a new creature."

"And so is the girl," said Mrs. Medlock. "She's becoming downright pretty. Her hair is thick and she has a rosy face. Those two children laugh like a pair of crazy ones. Perhaps they are growing fat on that."

"Perhaps they are," said the doctor. "Let them laugh."

The doctor and the nurse were not the only ones who had noticed a change in Colin. Mary, too, had noticed something different in Colin's room. She decided to say nothing that day, but she couldn't help staring at the picture over the mantel. The curtain had been drawn aside.

Colin had seen where Mary was looking. "I am going to keep the curtain like that," he said.

"Why?" Mary asked.

"Because it doesn't make me angry anymore to see my mother laughing. I awoke with the bright moonlight two nights ago and felt as if the magic was filling the room. A patch of moonlight was on the curtain, so I walked over and opened it. She looked as if she was laughing because she was glad I was standing. Now I want to see her laughing all the time."

"You are so like her picture now," said Mary, "that sometimes I think perhaps you are her ghost made into a boy."

"If I were her ghost, my father would be fond of me," Colin said.

~ 25 ~

"It's Mother!"

The children's belief in magic continued. Sometimes after their chanting in the morning, Colin would give them talks about magic.

Several weeks later, after one of his lectures, Colin was digging in the dirt in the garden. All of a sudden, he laid his trowel down, stood up, and threw out his arms wide. He had realized something.

"Mary, Dickon!" he cried out. "Just look at me! Do you remember the first morning you brought me here?"

They stopped their weeding and looked up at him.

"Aye," said Dickon.

"All at once I remembered it myself when I looked at my hand digging. I had to stand on my feet to see if it was real. And it is—I am well!" he said grandly. "And I shall live forever and ever!"

"You will," said Dickon and Mary together. They took in the sight of the strong, healthy boy in front of them.

But as Colin looked across the garden, the expression on his face changed. "Who is coming in here?" he asked.

The door in the ivy wall was pushed open and a woman entered. Her fresh face smiled across the greenery. Dickon's own eyes lit up like lamps. "It's Mother!" he cried. He ran across the grass to her. "I told her where to come."

Colin held out his hand to Mrs. Sowerby. "I had wanted to see you," he said. "You and Dickon and the secret garden."

The sight of Colin's healthy face brought a change in her own face. The corners of Mrs. Sowerby's mouth shook and her eyes looked misty. "Eh! Dear lad!" she said shakily.

"Are you surprised because I am so well?" he asked.

"Aye, that I am!" she answered. "But you're so like your mother, it made my heart jump!"

"Do you think that will make my father like me?" he said.

"Aye, for sure, lad," she answered, and gave his shoulder a soft pat.

Then Mrs. Sowerby put both hands on Mary's shoulders and looked into her face. "An' you, too!" she said. "I'll warrant you are like your mother, as well. We heard she was a beautiful woman. You will be like a blush rose when you grow up."

Mrs. Sowerby went around the garden with them and heard how each tree and plant had come alive. And they told her how hard it was pretending Colin was still an invalid.

Mrs. Sowerby laughed. "You won't have to keep it up much longer," she said. "Master Craven will come home."

"Do you think he will?" asked Colin eagerly. "I

couldn't bear it if any one else told him. I've been plan-ning it. I think I will just run into his room."

"I'd like to see his face, lad," Mrs. Sowerby said.

When Mrs. Sowerby got up to leave, Colin stood close to her. "You are just—just what I wanted," he said. "I wish you were my mother as well as Dickon's!"

Mrs. Sowerby bent down all at once and closed her arms around Colin. The mist swept over her eyes. "Eh! Dear lad!" she said. "Your own mother's in this garden, I believe. She couldn't keep out of it. Your father must come back to you—he must!"

In the Garden

While the secret garden was coming alive and the two children were coming alive with it, Mr. Craven was wandering around beautiful, faraway places. He was a man who had kept his mind filled with dark, heartbroken thoughts for ten years. A terrible sadness stayed with him.

A strange thing happened to Mr. Craven one day. He was in a lovely valley in Austria when he sat down by a stream. He let his mind go quiet and he began to notice the beauty of the sparkling water and the flowers by the stream. It had been ten years since he had noticed such things.

Mr. Craven sat there for a few minutes. "What is it?" he whispered to himself. "I almost feel as if I were alive!" He remembered this strange moment and the hour of it months afterward. When he was at Misselthwaite again, he discovered that on this same day Colin had cried out in the secret garden, "I am going to live forever and ever!" Slowly, very slowly, though he did not know it at the time, Mr. Craven was "coming alive" with the garden.

He began to think of Misselthwaite and whether he should return home. And then Mr. Craven had a dream. It was so real that he did not feel he was dreaming. "Archie! Archie!" a sweet voice said. His wife's voice was happy and sounded faraway. But he heard it as clearly as if it had been by his side.

"Lilias!" he answered, "Lilias, where are you?"

"In the garden," the voice said back. "In the garden!"

And then the dream ended. When Mr. Craven awoke, a servant was by his bed, holding a plate with several letters on it.

"In the garden," Mr. Craven said aloud, wondering to himself. "But the door is locked and the key is buried."

When he glanced at the letters a few minutes later, he saw that one was from Yorkshire. He opened it and the first words attracted his attention at once.

Dear Sir:

I am Susan Sowerby that spoke to you once on the moor about Miss Mary. Please, sir, I would come home if I were you. I think you would be glad to come and—if you will excuse me, sir—I think your lady would ask you to come if she were here.

—Susan Sowerby

Mr. Craven read the letter twice. "I will go back to Misselthwaite at once," he said.

In a few days, Mr. Craven was in Yorkshire again. On his journey back, he found himself thinking of his boy as he had never before. He remembered the days when he raved like a madman because the child was

85

alive and the mother was dead. He had not meant to be a bad father. He had simply not felt like a father at all. The boy's eyes looked so much like his wife's. But they were so unhappy that he could not bear to look at them.

Perhaps I have been wrong all these years, he thought. *It may be too late to do anything—quite too late.* He wondered if Susan Sowerby had written to him because the boy was much worse and was near death.

When Mr. Craven arrived at the manor, he went straight to the library and asked for Mrs. Medlock.

"How is Master Colin?" he said to her.

"Well, sir," she answered. "He's—he's different. Neither the doctor nor the nurse can figure him out."

"He has become more peculiar?" Mr. Craven asked.

"Yes, sir. Not long after his worst tantrum, he suddenly insisted on being taken out every day in the garden with Mary and Dickon, who pushes his chair."

"How does he look?" he asked.

"If he ate well, you'd think he was putting on healthy weight," she said. "And he laughs when he's alone with Miss Mary. He never used to laugh at all. The doctor has never been so puzzled in his life."

"Where is Master Colin now?" he said.

"In the garden, sir," she said. "He's always in the garden."

Mr. Craven's mind echoed with her last words. After Mrs. Medlock left, he repeated it again and again. "In the garden! In the garden!"

Mr. Craven left the house and walked through the garden with the fountain. He crossed the lawn and turned onto the long walk. He knew where the door was and stopped in front of it. But he did not know where the key was buried.

As he stood there, he heard sounds inside the garden. *Am I dreaming?* he wondered. They were the sounds of scuffling feet, lowered voices, and smothered joyous cries.

The feet ran faster and faster—they were nearing the garden door. Then the door was flung open wide, the sheet of ivy swung back, and a boy burst through it at full speed. Without seeing the outsider, he dashed into his arms.

When Mr. Craven looked at the boy, he gasped for breath.

He was a tall boy and a handsome one. He was glowing with life and his running had sent pink color to his face. The boy lifted a pair of gray eyes to him— eyes full of boyish laughter and rimmed with black lashes. It was the eyes that made Mr. Craven gasp.

"Who—what? Who!" he stammered.

This was not what Colin planned or had expected. And yet to come dashing out—winning a race—perhaps it was even better. Colin stood up straight and tall.

"Father," he said, "I am Colin. Perhaps you can't believe it. I scarcely can myself. I am Colin."

"In the garden!" Mr. Craven said. "In the garden!"

"Yes," Colin said. "It was the garden that did it—

and Mary and Dickon and the creatures and the magic. We kept it a secret until you came." Then he stood even taller. "I am well!"

He said it so much like a healthy boy with the words tumbling out in his eagerness that Mr. Craven's soul shook with unbelievable joy.

Colin put his hand on his father's arm. "Aren't you glad, father? I'm going to live forever and ever!"

Mr. Craven put his hands on the boy's shoulders and dared not say a word at that moment. After a minute, he spoke. "Take me into the garden, son, and tell me all about it."

And so they led him in. The place was a mass of autumn gold and purple and violet blue. And on every side there were lilies. Mr. Craven remembered when they had first been planted. He looked around and around just as the children had done when they first entered the garden themselves.

"I thought it would be dead," he said.

"Mary thought so, too," said Colin. "But it came alive."

Then the group sat down under their tree, but Colin stood to tell the whole story to his father. It was the strangest story Mr. Craven had ever heard. With mystery and magic and creatures, the strange midnight meeting, and the coming of spring. The playacting and the great secret so carefully kept. The listener laughed until tears came to his eyes. Colin was an athlete, a lecturer, a scientific discoverer, and a laughable, lovable, healthy young boy.

"Now," said Colin when he finished the story, "it

need not be a secret any more. I am never going to get into that chair again. I shall walk back to the house with you, Father."

Ben Weatherstaff's duties rarely took him away from the gardens, but on this day he made up an excuse to carry some vegetables to the kitchen. So, he was on the spot—where he hoped to be—when the most exciting event at Misselthwaite Manor happened.

"Did you see Master Craven and Master Colin?" Mrs. Medlock asked.

"Aye, that I did," he answered.

"What did they say to each other?" she said.

"I didn't hear that," said Ben. "But I'll tell you this. There's been goings-on outside this house people knows nothing about. An' you will find out soon."

Moments later, he waved his hand solemnly toward the window. "Look," he said. "Look what's comin' across the grass."

When Mrs. Medlock looked, she threw up her hands and gave a shriek. Every man and woman in the servants' hall came to look through the windows with their eyes wide.

Across the lawn came the master of Misselthwaite and he looked the way many had never seen him. And by his side with his head in the air and his eyes full of laughter walked strongly and steadily as any boy in Yorkshire—

Master Colin!